THE LAST CHANCE HOTEL

A SHORT STORY

ISAIAH YOUNG

The Last Chance Hotel
Copyright © 2025 by Isaiah Young.

MILTON & HUGO L.L.C.
4407 Park Ave., Suite 5
Union City, NJ 07087, USA

Website: *www. miltonandhugo.com*
Hotline: *1- 888-778-0033*
Email: *info@miltonandhugo.com*

Ordering Information:
Quantity sales. Special discounts are granted to corporations, associations, and other organizations. For more information on these discounts, please reach out to the publisher using the contact information provided above.

Library of Congress Control Number: 2025904674
ISBN-13: 979-8-89285-496-2 [Paperback Edition]
          979-8-89285-497-9 [Hardback Edition]
          979-8-89285-498-6 [Digital Edition]

Rev. date: 02/20/2025

PROLOGUE

Life. Death. It's the inevitable cycle we humans are bound to. One day, you're born, and after you've lived your life—however long or short—you pass on to whatever lies beyond. It's a truth we all face, yet one shrouded in mystery. No one who has crossed over has ever truly returned to tell the tale.

The afterlife is an enigma. Is it paradise? Darkness? A realm of infinite possibilities? For the living, it's a question that lingers just out of reach, an answer we hope to delay for as long as possible. But for the dead, it's reality.

When life ends, some souls leave Earth with peace in their hearts, their burdens lifted, and their regrets resolved. Others, however, carry the weight of their guilt, their missed chances, and their unspoken words. What becomes of them? Are they doomed to wander eternity shackled to the pain of their unfinished lives? Or is there something more?

What if—just once—you were given a chance to make it right? To see how your life could have unfolded if you'd made different choices, taken the chances you'd let slip by, or mended the broken pieces you left behind?

Welcome to the Last Chance Hotel. A place like no other. Here, you'll confront the life you've lived, the roads you didn't take, and the person you could have been.

Your regrets, your guilt, your unspoken dreams—all of it waits for you beyond these doors. So, what are you waiting for? Step inside and take a peek at what your life could have been.

GONE IN AN INSTANT

Ringgggg! Ringgggg! The sharp buzz of my phone rattling on the nightstand dragged me from my slumber. My hand fumbled for it, knocking over a half-empty water bottle in the process. Finally, I answered without looking at the caller ID.

"Arlo! You're late again!" my boss roared through the speaker. "Second time this week! What's the excuse this time?"

Still groggy, I rubbed my eyes. "Ugh, sorry, sir. Overslept. I'll be there ASAP."

"You'd better be," he barked. "Don't let this happen again." The line went dead.

I let out a long, frustrated groan and dropped the phone on the bed. "I'm so getting fired," I muttered. With a resigned sigh, I dragged myself up, the silence of my small house pressing in around me. It was always quiet—just me and my regrets.

I shuffled to the bathroom, the cold tiles jolting me awake. The face staring back at me in the mirror looked worn-out: heavy bags under my eyes, a few more gray strands in my hair. Another deep sigh escaped my lips. I brushed my teeth, splashed water on my face, and threw on my work uniform.

Grabbing my keys, I stepped out into the crisp morning air. My car, a green-and-black Mustang GT, gleamed faintly under the soft glow of the rising sun. Starting the engine, I felt a brief thrill as it roared to life. I pulled out of the driveway and muttered to myself, "Guess I'll be skipping breakfast again."

With the clock ticking, I pressed harder on the gas, pushing my speed past the limit. The quiet hum of the highway filled the air as I merged onto it. That's when I noticed the swerving 18-wheeler in my rearview mirror. Its movements were erratic, its acceleration unsettling.

The truck veered closer, the glint of its chrome grill filling my side mirror. My pulse quickened. "What's this guy doing?" I muttered. I switched lanes, but it stayed with me, now running parallel. That's when I saw the driver—head slumped forward, eyes closed. My breath caught. He was asleep.

The next moments blurred into chaos. The truck veered sharply, smashing into the side of my car. The world spun as I lost control. My Mustang flipped, metal screeching and glass shattering. Flames licked the edges of my vision as the car ignited. The last thing I saw was the blinding explosion before everything went black.

Darkness. Silence. Was this it? Did I just die?

THE GATE

Nothing but darkness stretched before me. Then, like a thunderclap, I was propelled forward, hurtling through a sea of stars. Memories unfolded around me—snippets of my life playing out in rapid succession. There I was as a baby, giggling at my mother's silly faces. Then a boy on a bike, scrapes on my knees and tears in my eyes. High school Arlo, grinning awkwardly at prom. Adult Arlo, alone in his empty apartment. The moments streamed past, culminating in the fiery crash that ended it all.

And then I stopped.

A glowing path materialized beneath me, stretching toward an enormous gate. The gate shimmered with an ethereal blue light, intricate carvings adorning its surface. At its center stood a figure cloaked in a robe of the same radiant hue. In one hand, he held a staff tipped with a glowing crystal. He exuded a presence that was both calming and commanding.

I stood, my body feeling lighter than air. Tentatively, I began to walk the path, each step echoing in the vast expanse of silence. The robed man watched me approach, unmoving. When I finally stood before him, I hesitated.

"Who are you?" I asked, my voice trembling.

He didn't answer immediately. Instead, he raised the staff, and the gate pulsed with light. Finally, he spoke, his voice deep and resonant. "You cannot pass."

I blinked. "What? Why not?"

"Your soul is burdened," he said simply. "Regret clings to you, tethering you to the life you left behind. Until you let go, the gate will remain closed to you."

"So what am I supposed to do?" I asked, desperation creeping into my voice.

The man gestured to the side, and the path shifted, revealing a massive structure in the distance. It was a hotel, towering and ornate, with lights glowing warmly from every window. Vines crept up its walls, alive and writhing like serpents. Birds circled its spires, their cries echoing faintly.

"That is the Last Chance Hotel," the man explained. "Within its walls, you will confront the moments that weigh on your soul. Behind its doors lies the opportunity to reconcile with your past and understand the life you could have had. But be warned: the choices you make there will not alter your reality. They are but glimpses of what could have been."

"And if I don't go?" I asked.

The man's expression darkened. With a wave of his staff, a portal opened beside him. Inside was an endless void, black and empty, save for the faint outlines of wandering souls. They drifted aimlessly, silent and alone.

"Your other option is the void," he said. "An eternity of nothingness."

I stared into the void, a chill running down my spine. "I'll go to the hotel," I said quickly.

The man nodded and struck the ground with his staff. The path shifted again, leading directly to the hotel's grand entrance.

"This is where we part ways," he said. "The rest is up to you."

Before I could respond, he vanished. Taking a deep breath, I stepped forward and opened the door to the Last Chance Hotel.

THE LAST CHANCE HOTEL

The lobby of the Last Chance Hotel took my breath away. Enormous chandeliers hung from a ceiling so high it felt like a cathedral, their crystals refracting light in a thousand directions. The air smelled faintly of lavender and something warm and earthy, like freshly polished wood. Birds fluttered above, their wings catching golden rays filtering through stained glass windows. Vines twisted elegantly along the marble walls, their leaves glimmering as though alive. Everything about the place felt surreal, like stepping into a dream.

I wandered further inside, my footsteps echoing on the gleaming floor. Plush chairs and ornate couches were arranged in cozy clusters, inviting visitors to sit and stay awhile. Beyond the lobby stretched a hallway lined with countless doors, each glowing faintly with a soft, otherworldly light.

I was so lost in awe that I didn't notice the man until I practically walked into him. He wore a perfectly tailored tuxedo, his bright brown eyes sparkling with a mischievous glint. His curly hair framed a youthful, charming face that seemed both familiar and utterly strange.

"Whoa there, Arlo!" he said, straightening his jacket with a grin. "Careful where you're going. You might end up through a door you're not ready for."

I took a step back, startled. "I'm sorry, do I know you?"

The man's grin widened. "Not yet, but you will. I'm your guide. You can call me... Guide." He extended a hand, and after a moment of hesitation, I shook it. His grip was warm and steady, reassuring in a way I couldn't quite explain.

"Guide? That's it?" I asked.

"That's all you need to know for now," he replied. "I'm here to help you navigate your journey through the Last Chance Hotel. Think of me as your concierge, your coach, your occasional therapist— whatever you need."

I glanced around at the glowing doors. "And what exactly is my journey?"

Guide's expression grew more serious. "Each of these doors represents a moment from your life. A choice, a regret, a crossroads you never fully came to terms with. Your job is to step through, confront what's inside, and come out the other side a little lighter."

"And if I don't?" I asked, a nervous knot forming in my stomach.

Guide shrugged. "Then you stay here. Forever. But let's not dwell on that, shall we? The first door's this way."

He gestured to a door marked with a glowing number 1. My heart pounded as I approached it. Whatever lay beyond, I knew one thing for certain—there was no turning back.

WHERE IT ALL BEGAN

I placed my hand on the door's cool, brass handle, feeling the weight of the moment settle in my chest. Taking a deep breath, I twisted the knob and stepped through.

The air around me shifted instantly, cool and crisp as if I'd walked into another world. My feet hit solid ground, and I blinked against the sudden brightness. I stood in what looked like my old elementary school playground, every detail painfully familiar—the rusting jungle gym, the worn swings creaking in the breeze, the faint scent of freshly cut grass mixed with the tang of chalk dust from nearby classrooms.

My heart sank as I realized where I was. This memory had been buried deep, but it resurfaced with startling clarity. There, by the swings, was a younger version of me, no more than eight years old. I watched as he swung back and forth, a determined scowl on his face. Then I saw her—a little girl with pigtails and a bright yellow dress, walking up to him nervously.

"Hey, can I have a turn?" she asked, her voice soft but hopeful.

Young me glared at her. "No, I was here first!" he snapped, kicking the ground to swing higher.

The girl's face fell, but she didn't back away. "You've been on for a long time. It's my favorite swing. Can't we share?"

"I said no!" Young me shouted. Then, without thinking, he shoved her backward. She stumbled, falling to the ground and scraping her knee. Tears welled up in her eyes as a teacher rushed over.

I winced, shame washing over me as I watched the scene unfold. The teacher scolded young me, dragging him off the swing and toward the school building. The girl was left crying on the ground, clutching her scraped knee.

I wanted to scream at my younger self, to shake him and ask why he'd been so cruel. But I knew the answer. Even at eight years old, I'd already started building walls, pushing people away before they could hurt me. It was a pattern that would follow me for years.

Guide's voice broke through my thoughts. "You can change this, Arlo. You don't have to carry it with you anymore."

I turned to see him standing beside me, his expression calm but expectant. "How?" I asked.

"Step in," he said simply, gesturing toward the scene. "Be the person you wish you'd been."

I hesitated, then nodded. Steeling myself, I stepped forward and into my younger self. The sensation was strange, like slipping into a suit that was both too small and too familiar. I was eight years old again, sitting on the swing, my legs dangling above the ground.

The girl stood before me, her hopeful eyes watching me closely. I felt the anger and defensiveness rising, the instinct to push her away. But this time, I stopped myself. Instead, I slowed the swing to a stop and hopped off.

"Here," I said, offering her the swing. "You can have a turn."

Her face lit up with surprise and gratitude. "Really? Thanks!" She climbed onto the swing, gripping the chains tightly as she began to pump her legs. Her laughter filled the air, light and joyful.

The weight in my chest lifted, replaced by a warmth I hadn't felt in years. As the door to the playground memory faded into white, I was swept through a stream of new images. I saw myself and the girl, laughing together as we shared the swings after school. Another memory surfaced when we were a little older, sitting under a tree in the park, exchanging stories about our dreams. She was more than the girl I had once pushed away; she was my best friend now. Her laughter echoed in my mind, and the warmth of those moments filled the void I hadn't realized was there before.

For the first time in so long, I felt what it meant to truly have someone by my side.

The new memories began to dissolve, and I stepped back out into the hallway of the Last Chance Hotel. The door behind me glowed faintly, it's light soft, and warm.

Guide smiled. "Well done. Ready for the next one?"

I'M SORRY, MOM

"Wow," I muttered under my breath. The sheer weight of what I had experienced behind Door 1 left me reeling. I never thought I'd be able to see my life change before my eyes like that. And yet, it had. Little did I know that revisiting and changing that memory would end up being so rewarding. I finally stood up from the floor, taking a deep, steadying breath. My head was spinning, my heart still heavy. Knowing that I could have had a best friend in life if I'd just opened myself up—that knowledge was a lot to take in.

The Guide watched me closely. "Do you feel ready for Door 2?" he asked, his voice calm but expectant.

I looked at him, dazed. "Man, I'm not sure. Door 1 was a lot to take in."

The Guide smiled, and to my surprise, he started laughing. It wasn't a soft chuckle—this was a hearty, full-bodied laugh that echoed through the hallway. Confused, I stared at him.

"What's so funny?" I asked, my frustration bubbling up.

His laughter faded, though the grin remained. "If you think Door 1 was wild, you've got a long journey ahead of you, my friend."

I sighed, shaking my head. "Whatever. Let's get this over with. I guess I'm ready for Door 2."

The Guide nodded and pointed toward the next glowing door. A shimmering number "2" was etched into the surface, pulsing gently. "You know the drill," he said.

I hesitated, staring at the door. My mind was racing. What could possibly be behind this one? Whatever it was, I knew I wasn't ready. Still, I forced my feet to move. I approached the door slowly, gripping the handle with a trembling hand.

"Here goes nothing," I murmured. And with that, I stepped through.

I fell. It wasn't like a stumble or a trip; this was a free-fall, plunging through an endless void. When I finally landed, I found myself in my old apartment. The air was heavy, tinged with the faint smell of lavender cleaning spray—Mom's favorite. The room was dim and quiet, filled with a hollow kind of loneliness.

I floated in my spirit form, observing the scene before me. It was surreal seeing my younger teenage self sitting on the couch. He had the same sad look in his eyes that I remembered all too well. He was slumped over, a bowl of instant ramen in his hand, watching an episode of *Ninjago* on Cartoon Network. The sight tugged at my heart.

The door creaked open, and Mom walked in, still wearing her scrubs from the hospital. She looked exhausted, her smile strained but genuine. "Hey, kiddo! Sorry, I'm home so late. The hospital had me stay a little longer for an emergency."

Teenage me barely glanced at her. His disappointment was palpable. "You say that every time, Mom. It's 11 PM! Is work really that important to you?"

Her face fell, the corners of her eyes glistening with unshed tears. She set her bag down and sat next to him on the couch. Reaching for the remote, she muted the TV. "Look, kiddo, I know I'm not home as much as I should be, and I'm sorry for that. Trust me, I'd rather be here with you, watching you grow up. But it's been hard taking care of everything on my own. I want you to know that I'm trying. I love you, Arlo. More than anything in the world."

But teenage me didn't care. He was already upset, his emotions boiling over. He slammed the bowl of ramen onto the table, his eyes brimming with tears of frustration. "I hate you! My life has been nothing but miserable because of you!"

With that, he stormed off to his room, slamming the door shut. Mom stayed on the couch, stunned. Her hands trembled as she buried her face in them, her quiet sobs breaking the silence of the apartment. "I'm a terrible mother," she whispered to herself.

As I floated there, watching this unfold, my chest tightened. I wanted to reach out to her, to tell her it wasn't true. That she'd done everything she could. But I could only watch.

Later that night, Mom knocked on teenage me's door, but there was no response. Worried, she opened it and found the room empty. The window was open, curtains billowing in the night breeze. Panic set in as she grabbed her phone and called 911 to report me missing.

But then—it happened. She clutched her chest, gasping for air. Her legs gave out, and she collapsed onto the floor. She was having a heart attack.

Meanwhile, teenage me was wandering the streets, lost and crying. I stopped at a gas station, buying a piece of candy with the spare change in my pocket. Eating it calmed me down, and I decided to go back home, realizing how foolish I'd been.

When I arrived, the sight of flashing lights greeted me. Two cop cars and an ambulance were parked outside the apartment building. I ran up the stairs, panic flooding my veins. Two officers were standing outside our door.

"Are you Arlo?" one of them asked. I didn't respond. I pushed past them, only to see EMTs surrounding Mom's lifeless body. They were performing CPR, but she wasn't responding.

I froze, unable to process what was happening. My knees gave out as one of the officers covered my eyes and led me away. That was the last time I saw my mom before I was sent to foster care.

The memory was agonizing to relive, even as a spectator. Tears streamed down my face as I floated above it all. But I wasn't going to let this be the end. I reached out my hand, turning it to the left, reversing the memory. Time rewound, the scene blurring until I was back on the couch, eating ramen and watching cartoons.

I floated closer to teenage me, and just like before, I was pulled into my younger body. When Mom walked through the door this time, everything was different.

"Hey, kiddo! Sorry, I'm home so late. The hospital had me stay a little longer for an emergency," she said.

I looked up, smiling warmly. "Hey, Mom. It's good to see you. I missed you."

Her eyes widened in surprise before she teared up, a big smile spreading across her face. "I missed you too, kiddo."

She put her bag down and sat next to me on the couch. "I know I haven't been around much, and I'm sorry. It's been hard doing this on my own, but I'm trying my best. I was thinking... I have

Saturday off. How about we go get ice cream? Spend the whole day together?"

I hugged her tightly, tears streaming down my face. "You're the best mom in the world. I'd love that."

We spent the rest of the evening watching cartoons, laughing, and eating ramen. For the first time, the apartment felt warm—filled with love. When I was finally pushed out of the memory, back into the glowing expanse of the hotel's hallway, I felt a sense of peace I hadn't known in years.

As I floated through the cosmos of my memories, I saw glimpses of what could have been: Mom cheering me on at graduation, laughing with me at family dinners, and standing proudly by my side as I achieved my dreams. It was bittersweet, but it reminded me to cherish what I'd had, even if only for a moment.

Guide was waiting for me as I emerged, his expression softer than usual. "Well done, Arlo," he said.

I wiped my eyes, nodding. "Thanks. I just wish I could have told her goodbye."

"You did more than that," Guide replied. "You gave her the love she deserved. That's all any of us can do."

IT'S THE LITTLE THINGS

The third door glowed faintly, its surface smooth and polished, as if untouched by the passage of time. It was an unnerving contrast to the previous doors, which bore the marks of pain and struggle. This one looked deceptively inviting, yet the unease in my chest grew stronger with each step I took toward it.

"This one's different," I muttered aloud, glancing at Guide.

He nodded, his expression neutral but watchful. "Every door is different, Arlo. But you're right—this one isn't about what you did. It's about what you didn't do."

I hesitated, my hand hovering over the brass handle. "What's that supposed to mean?"

Guide's eyes softened, a rare flicker of emotion crossing his face. "Sometimes, the hardest regrets to face aren't about the mistakes you made. They're about the opportunities you let slip away."

I swallowed hard, his words sinking in. Slowly, I pushed the door open.

The air shifted as I stepped through, warm and tinged with the faint aroma of vanilla and old books. I was in a cozy bookstore, its shelves crammed with worn paperbacks and pristine hardcovers. The sunlight streamed through large windows, casting golden patterns across the wooden floor. A sense of calm washed over me, but it was laced with an undercurrent of something bittersweet.

I knew this place. It was where Juniper and I had spent countless afternoons, back when the world seemed full of possibilities. My gaze landed on a younger version of myself, seated at a small table near the back of the store. I was scribbling furiously in a notebook, a half-finished coffee growing cold beside me.

"Arlo," Juniper's voice called, light and teasing. She emerged from behind a bookshelf, holding up a novel. Her eyes sparkled with excitement. "Look at this! It's the one I've been telling you about—the one with the poet who moves to Paris."

My younger self barely glanced up, muttering, "That's great, Juni."

The light in her expression dimmed slightly, but she masked it with a smile. "You've been working on that all day," she said, setting the book down. "Come on, take a break. Let's go for a walk. It's beautiful outside."

"Can't," he replied curtly, his pen never pausing. "I'm on a roll."

I winced, remembering this moment all too well. She had tried so hard to reach me, to pull me out of my head, but I had been too wrapped up in my own ambitions to notice.

Juniper hesitated, her hands fidgeting with the edges of the book. "Arlo," she said softly, "I know your writing is important to you. But I'm here too. Can we just... have one day? One afternoon?"

My younger self sighed, finally looking up. His face was lined with frustration, but beneath it was something else—guilt. "Juniper, you don't get it. If I don't put in the work now, nothing will ever happen for me. I can't afford to take a break."

She nodded slowly, her smile fading. "Okay," she said quietly. "I'll see you later, then."

As she walked away, the memory froze, leaving me staring at the image of her retreating back.

"Why am I seeing this?" I asked aloud, my voice thick with emotion. "Out of all the things I've done, this... this doesn't seem like it should matter so much."

Guide's voice came from behind me, calm but firm. "That's the thing about regret. Sometimes it's not the big moments that haunt us. It's the small ones—the times when we didn't show up for the people who mattered most."

I felt the weight of his words settle over me. "Can I change it?" I asked, turning toward him.

He shook his head. "You know the answer to that, Arlo. But you can face it. And maybe that's enough."

I looked back at Juniper, frozen mid-step. Slowly, I approached my younger self, stepping into his place. The weight of his ambition and self-doubt hit me like a tidal wave, but I pushed through it.

When Juniper turned to leave, I called after her. "Wait, Juni."

She stopped, her shoulders tense. "What?"

I stood, leaving the notebook behind. "You're right. Let's go for a walk."

Her eyes widened in surprise. "Really?"

"Yeah," I said, a small smile breaking through. "This can wait. You can't."

Her smile returned, bright and full of hope. She reached for my hand, and as our fingers intertwined, the bookstore dissolved around us, leaving only warmth and light.

When I opened my eyes, I was back in the hallway. The third door was closed behind me, its glow steady and soft.

Guide was waiting, his expression unreadable. "Look at you getting it," he said quietly.

I nodded, the ache in my chest giving way to something lighter. "I think I'm finally starting to understand."

"Good," Guide said, gesturing to the next door. "Because it's not over yet."

I took a deep breath and stepped forward.

THE PRICE OF A KISS

The fourth door loomed ahead of me, larger and more imposing than the previous ones. Its surface was weathered, marked with deep grooves as if something had clawed at it in desperation. A faint, uneven glow pulsed around the frame, casting flickering shadows on the dim hallway walls. My breath hitched as I approached. The air here felt heavier, charged with an ominous tension.

"Are you sure you're ready for this one?" Guide's voice startled me. He stood leaning casually against the wall, but his usual playful demeanor was gone. His expression was serious, almost sad.

"Do I have a choice?" I asked, though I already knew the answer.

Guide sighed, his eyes meeting mine. "Not really. But be warned—this one's going to hurt. It's tied to something you've buried so deeply, you've barely allowed yourself to remember it."

My chest tightened, fear curling in my gut. I nodded, swallowing hard. "Let's do this."

Guide stepped back as I gripped the cold iron handle and pushed the door open. A gust of humid air hit me, thick with the scent of rain-soaked earth and ozone. I stepped through and found myself back in the hallways of my high school. The fluorescent lights overhead buzzed faintly, and the faint smell of cleaning solution and teenage sweat hung in the air. My stomach twisted into knots as the memories came rushing back.

I was now in spirit form, floating through the familiar corridors. Locker doors slammed shut in the distance, and snippets of conversation echoed around me. I spotted my younger self walking hand in hand with Juniper. She was radiant, just as I remembered her—her light blue highlights framing her black hair perfectly, and her hazel eyes sparkling with warmth. Seeing her again made my chest ache.

Younger me was smiling as they walked, leaning close to whisper something in her ear that made her laugh. It was a sound that seemed to brighten the entire hallway. I followed them as they stopped outside Juniper's classroom.

"I'll see you after class," younger me said, giving her hand a gentle squeeze.

Juniper smiled. "Before I go, there's something I want to say." She hesitated, her expression turning serious. "I've been hearing rumors about Zara. They say she has a crush on you. Just... be careful, okay?"

Younger me rolled his eyes but smiled reassuringly. "It's just a rumor, love. She doesn't seem interested in me from what I've seen."

Juniper nodded reluctantly. "Okay. But don't say I didn't warn you." She gave him a quick kiss before heading into her classroom, her smile lingering even as the door closed behind her.

I wanted to shout at my younger self, to warn him not to be so dismissive, but I knew it was useless. I watched as he turned and walked to his own classroom, completely unaware of the storm brewing.

The scene shifted slightly, and I followed younger me into his classroom. He made his way to the back, his favorite spot. Zara, who usually sat in the front, surprised him by sitting down right next to him.

"Hey, Arlo," she said with a playful smile. "How's it going?"

"It's going well," younger me replied, looking slightly puzzled. "Just a little tired, but I'm here."

"Aren't we all?" Zara said with a soft laugh, leaning in closer than necessary.

Class began, but Zara's attention was not on the lesson. Halfway through, she scribbled something on a piece of paper and slid it over to younger me. He hesitated before unfolding it.

Hey, I really need to talk to you about something, but I can't in class. Ask to go to the bathroom in a few minutes and meet me in the hallway. Kapeesh?

Younger me glanced at her, and she gave him a small, encouraging smile. Reluctantly, he nodded. A few minutes later, Zara raised her hand and asked to use the bathroom. Once she left, younger me waited for the teacher to look away before following her.

Zara was waiting just outside the classroom, leaning casually against the lockers. When she saw him, she grabbed his hand without a word and led him down the hallway to the stairwell. They walked down to the very bottom, a secluded area no one ever used. The air was cooler here, the faint hum of the building's ventilation system the only sound.

Younger me finally spoke. "Okay, so what's going on? What did you need to talk about?"

Zara turned to face him, her eyes locking onto his. "Arlo, I know you and Juniper are together, but... I need to be honest with you. I think you deserve better."

He frowned. "What do you mean?"

"She's not who you think she is," Zara said, stepping closer. "People are saying she's been talking to other guys behind your back. You shouldn't waste your time on someone who doesn't value you."

Younger me looked conflicted. "I don't know. I'll just talk to her and see what's going on."

Zara placed a hand on his chest, stopping him. "No, wait. That's not all. Just... close your eyes."

He hesitated. "Why?"

"Trust me," she said softly, her voice almost a whisper.

Younger me exhaled, unsure, but he closed his eyes. That's when Zara leaned in and kissed him. It wasn't tentative or gentle—it was bold, almost desperate. She pressed him against the wall, her hands sliding up to his shoulders. For a moment, younger me froze, but then he kissed her back, the heat of the moment clouding his judgment.

The kiss deepened, their breaths mingling as the world around them seemed to blur. Zara's hands gripped his shirt, pulling him closer, and younger me responded, his own hands finding her waist. The intensity of it was electric, intoxicating, and utterly wrong.

Then the stairwell door creaked open.

"Arlo?"

Juniper's voice cut through the haze like a blade. Both of them froze, their lips still inches apart. Slowly, they turned to see her standing at the top of the stairs, her hazel eyes wide with shock and betrayal. Tears welled up in her eyes as she took a shaky step back.

"Juniper, wait!" younger me shouted, pushing Zara away. But Juniper was already running, her sobs echoing through the stairwell.

Panic set in as younger me chased after her. The tornado warning blared over the intercom, its shrill tone adding to the chaos. Students and teachers shouted, scrambling to find shelter, but all younger me could think about was Juniper.

THE TORNADO OF REGRET

Beep! Beep! Beep! This is not a drill. Staff and students, seek shelter immediately!

The intercom blared as the hallway erupted into chaos. Teachers herded students into designated safety zones, but younger me was still chasing Juniper. He finally caught up to her near the end of the hallway, grabbing her arm.

"Juniper, please, let me explain!" he begged, his voice cracking.

She shook her head, tears streaming down her face. "There's nothing to explain, Arlo! I trusted you!"

Before he could respond, the lights flickered, and the ground began to tremble. The tornado was close. A teacher shouted, "Everyone, get down! Cover your heads!"

Younger me grabbed Juniper and pulled her to the ground, shielding her with his body as the storm roared closer. The lights above shattered, raining down glass as the wind howled through the building. Locker doors flew open, their contents scattered across the hallway. The deafening roar of the tornado consumed everything.

Suddenly, the wall at the far end of the hallway gave way, ripped apart by the force of the storm. Debris flew everywhere, narrowly missing the students who were huddled together. The wind pulled at Juniper's hair and clothes, her body lifting slightly off the ground.

Younger me held onto her with all his strength, his knuckles white as he gripped her arm.

"Arlo, you have to let me go!" Juniper screamed over the roar of the wind, her voice filled with desperation.

"No! I won't lose you!" he shouted back, tears streaming down his face.

The tornado drew closer, the suction growing stronger. A teacher nearby shouted, "Arlo, get to safety! You can't hold on much longer!"

Juniper looked into his eyes, her own filled with a heartbreaking mix of love and resignation. "Arlo, I love you. Please, live for me."

Her hand slipped from his grasp, and she was gone. The force of the tornado pulled her into its chaotic vortex, her figure disappearing in an instant.

Younger me collapsed to the floor, sobbing uncontrollably. A teacher grabbed him, pulling him toward the stairwell where the other students were sheltered. The group huddled together as the storm raged on, the building shaking with every gust. The sound was deafening, a cacophony of destruction that seemed endless.

When the tornado finally passed, the silence was almost worse. The hallway was unrecognizable, debris and rubble covering every surface. Younger me sat against the wall, his body shaking as he clutched Juniper's scarf, the only thing left of her.

The memory ended abruptly, leaving me back in the hallway of the Last Chance Hotel. My hands were shaking as I turned to Guide. "Why couldn't I stop it?" I asked, my voice barely a whisper.

Guide's expression was unreadable. "Not every memory is meant to be fixed, Arlo. Sometimes, the only way forward is to let go."

THE BETRAYAL

The fifth door loomed before me, its surface dull and unassuming, but there was a heaviness to it that made my chest tighten. I stared at the simple brass handle, my hand trembling as I reached for it.

Guide, as always, stood nearby. His presence was comforting, but his expression this time held something deeper—a kind of sadness. "This one," he said quietly, "will be one of the hardest to face."

"Why?" I asked, though I already felt the answer in the pit of my stomach.

"Because this memory isn't just about regret," Guide said. "It's about betrayal."

The word hit me like a punch. I nodded, my throat tight. "I'll face it," I said, though my voice wavered.

Guide stepped aside, and I pushed the door open.

The air was warm and crisp, filled with the scent of freshly baked dough and melted cheese. I was back on my college campus, walking through the quad alongside Theo, my best friend and roommate. We were both wearing lab coats, our notebooks tucked under our arms as we discussed our latest project.

Theo's excitement was infectious. "Arlo, just think about it. FlexForm Dynamics could change the world. Prosthetics that not only improve lives but save them—devices that monitor health, detect diseases early, and give people a second chance. We're going to revolutionize healthcare."

I grinned, clapping him on the back. "I know, Theo. And we'll do it together. You and me, co-founders of the next big thing."

Theo beamed, his confidence shining through. "We'll make it happen, Arlo. I know we will."

As we approached the campus pizzeria, the smell of grease and pepperoni wafted through the air, making my stomach growl. We grabbed a booth in the corner and ordered a large pizza to share. The place was bustling, filled with the hum of student chatter and the occasional clatter of plates.

Theo leaned back in his seat, a wide grin on his face. "Okay, Arlo. Once we get this prototype running, we'll present it to the board. They'll have to fund it."

"Absolutely," I said, raising my soda. "To FlexForm Dynamics."

"To FlexForm Dynamics," Theo echoed, clinking his cup against mine.

Our laughter was interrupted by a group entering the pizzeria. They were loud and boisterous, their presence commanding attention. At the front of the group was Tyler, a tall, broad-shouldered guy who practically radiated confidence. Behind him were two girls— Bianca, with jet-black hair and piercing green eyes, and Charlotte, a blonde with a smile that seemed to light up the room.

They ordered their pizza and, after a moment of hushed whispers, made their way to our table. Tyler was holding a stack of flyers, which he dropped onto the table with a cocky grin.

"Hey, fellas," Tyler said. "Big party at our house tonight. You should come. Drinks, music, good company." He gestured to Bianca and Charlotte, who both smiled.

Theo shook his head immediately. "Thanks, but we're good. We've got a lot of work to do."

Tyler's grin didn't falter. "Come on, man. Don't be lame. You could be hanging out with these two lovely ladies instead of crunching numbers all night."

Bianca tilted her head, giving Theo a playful smirk, while Charlotte's eyes locked onto mine. There was a challenge in her gaze, a silent dare.

Theo opened his mouth to refuse again, but I spoke up. "Actually, Theo, maybe we should go."

He turned to me, surprised. "What?"

I shrugged, forcing a casual tone. "Think about it. We've been grinding nonstop. A little recognition wouldn't hurt. People on campus barely know we exist. This could change that."

Theo hesitated, his brow furrowed. "I don't know, Arlo. We have so much to do."

"One night," I said, leaning forward. "It'll be fun. And who knows? Maybe it'll be good for us."

After a long pause, Theo sighed. "Okay. One night."

Tyler clapped him on the shoulder. "That's the spirit. See you tonight."

The group left, their laughter trailing behind them. Theo looked at me, still uncertain. "I hope you're right about this."

I forced a smile. "Trust me."

The memory shifted, and we were at the party. The house was packed, music thumping so loud I could feel it in my chest. Theo and I stood near the entrance, looking out of place in our neatly pressed shirts. Before long, Bianca and Charlotte found us.

Bianca took Theo's hand, leading him toward the dance floor. Charlotte looped her arm through mine, pulling me toward the staircase. "Let's find somewhere quieter," she said, her voice smooth and inviting.

She led me to a room upstairs, where Tyler was waiting. The grin on his face immediately put me on edge.

"Here's the deal," Tyler said, his tone casual but laced with malice. "Your buddy Theo tried to blow me off earlier, and I don't let stuff like that slide. So we're going to have a little fun with him."

I frowned. "What are you talking about?"

"A prank," Tyler said, holding up his phone. "Nothing serious. Just something to knock him down a peg. You help me, and I'll make sure you're taken care of." He pulled out a wad of cash. "Ten grand. And you get Charlotte. Sounds like a good deal, doesn't it?"

I hesitated, the weight of the decision pressing down on me. Part of me wanted to walk away, but another part—the part that craved recognition, and acceptance—wavered.

"Fine," I said finally, my voice hollow. "What do you want me to do?"

The prank played out like a nightmare. Tyler, Charlotte, and I hid in the closet while Bianca lured Theo into the room. She kept him distracted, whispering sweet nothings and coaxing him to undress. Then, at Tyler's signal, we burst out, phones recording as Theo scrambled to cover himself.

Tyler laughed, his voice cutting through Theo's humiliation. "Smile, buddy. You're going viral."

"What the hell?" I snapped, turning on Tyler. "You didn't say you'd post it."

Theo's eyes met mine, tears streaming down his face. "How could you?" he whispered. "I thought we were friends."

He ran from the room, and I chased after him, but he was gone. I sat on the curb outside the house, my chest heavy with regret. Charlotte came out, trying to comfort me, but her presence only made the guilt worse.

She took my hand, her touch light and inviting. "Come on," she said softly. "Let's go back inside."

Too emotionally drained to argue, I let her guide me back to the room. When we entered, Tyler and Bianca were already there, locked in a heated kiss. They broke apart when they noticed us, Tyler smirking as he slung an arm around Bianca's shoulders.

"You guys can have this room," Tyler said. "Have fun."

He and Bianca left, leaving Charlotte and me alone. She closed the door and locked it, her eyes meeting mine. There was a hunger in her gaze, an invitation I didn't have the strength to refuse.

We came together almost instinctively, her lips soft and insistent against mine. Clothes fell away piece by piece, and for a while, the guilt and shame were drowned out by the sensation of her touch. Her fingers trailed down my back, her breath hot against my neck as we moved together. It was intoxicating, and for a fleeting moment, I felt like I belonged.

But as the adrenaline faded and the room grew quiet, the weight of what I'd done crashed back down on me. Charlotte lay beside me, her head resting on my chest, but I couldn't find comfort in her presence. My mind was already on Theo—on the betrayal that had cost me my best friend.

The next morning, I woke to find Charlotte still asleep. I slipped out of bed, dressed quickly, and left the house. The cool morning air hit me like a slap as I made my way back to the dorm.

When I arrived, Theo's side of the room was empty. His belongings were gone, and a single note sat on his desk:

*Hey Arlo,

What you did last night was messed up. I hope you got what you wanted, but I feel very betrayed that you were in on that. You took part in humiliating me. I thought we were going to help the world together. Instead, you just hurt me. I've withdrawn from school and am transferring to a different one. Enjoy the dorm to yourself.

P.S. Theo*

I stared at the note, my heart breaking. I'd lost my best friend, my partner, the one person who believed in me. And for what? A fleeting sense of recognition?

Tears filled my eyes as the memory froze, the weight of it crushing. I felt my spectating self step forward, the Arlo outside the moment reaching in to fix what had been broken.

I raised my hand, and the scene began to rewind. Time flowed backward, the events playing in reverse like a film reel spinning out of control. The night dissolved, the party vanished, and soon I was back at the pizzeria, sitting across from Theo as Tyler approached our table.

This time, when Theo looked at me for guidance, I didn't hesitate.

"No thanks," I said firmly. "We're good."

Tyler shrugged, walking away. Theo smiled, relief evident on his face. "Thanks, Arlo," he said. "Let's get back to work."

As the memory dissolved, I was pulled into a whirlwind of vibrant, new memories, ones that hadn't existed before. I saw Theo and me standing in a sleek, glass-walled office with "Flexform Dynamics" proudly displayed on the wall behind us. We were older, but the spark in Theo's eyes was the same.

Another memory came rushing in: we were at a hospital, presenting a prototype prosthetic to a young girl who had lost her leg. The device wasn't just functional; it was revolutionary, equipped to monitor her health and keep her safe. Her wide-eyed smile was something I would never forget.

More images followed, Theo giving a speech at a conference, the two of us shaking hands with world leaders, and a factory producing our devices that would help millions of people. I saw us laughing over pizza in the office, just like we had dreamed back in college.

This was the life we were supposed to have. Together. And it was beautiful.

The new memories dissolved for good this time, leaving me standing in the hallway of the Last Chance Hotel. The fifth door stood closed behind me, its dull surface now glowing faintly, as if healed.

Guide was waiting, his expression calm but knowing. "Well done," he said.

I nodded, the weight in my chest finally beginning to lift. "I think I'm ready for the next door."

THE MIRROR ROOM

The sixth door wasn't like the others. It shimmered faintly, as if it were made of liquid silver, rippling under an unseen breeze. Its surface reflected a distorted version of the hallway, bending and warping reality in ways that made my stomach churn.

Guide stood silently beside me, his usual calm demeanor replaced with a look of quiet apprehension.

"This one feels… wrong," I said, my voice hesitant.

"It's not wrong," Guide replied softly. "But it is different. You're not stepping into a memory this time. You're stepping into yourself."

I frowned. "What does that mean?"

Guide's gaze was steady, unwavering. "You'll see."

I didn't like the cryptic response, but at this point, I didn't have a choice. Taking a deep breath, I pressed my hand against the rippling surface of the door. It gave way like water, cool and fluid against my skin, and before I knew it, I was pulled through.

The world on the other side was nothing like the memories I'd walked through before. There was no distinct setting, no tangible place to orient myself. Instead, I stood in a vast, empty expanse of gray mist that seemed to stretch endlessly in every direction. The air was still, almost oppressively so, and the silence pressed against my ears like a physical weight.

Then, out of the mist, a shape began to emerge. At first, it was vague and indistinct, but as it drew closer, I realized it was a figure. My heart sank when I saw who it was.

It was me.

Not the younger version of me that I'd seen in the other doors, but the person I was now. The man who had walked into the Last Chance Hotel burdened with regrets and mistakes. He stood there, staring at me with an expression I couldn't quite read.

"So this is it," he said, his voice identical to mine. "The big confrontation."

"What are you?" I asked, my voice barely above a whisper.

He smirked, but there was no humor in it. "I'm you. Or at least, I'm the part of you you've been avoiding all this time. The part you don't want to face."

A chill ran down my spine. "Why now? Why here?"

"Because you're almost at the end," he said, taking a step closer. "And before you can move on, you have to face the truth. All of it."

I took a step back instinctively, but there was nowhere to go. The mist seemed to close in around us, cutting off any escape.

"What truth?" I demanded, my voice shaking.

He tilted his head, studying me like I was some sort of puzzle. "The truth about who you are. The truth about why you ended up here. You've been telling yourself it's all about your regrets— Juniper, your mom, Theo. And yeah, those things matter. But there's more to it than that, isn't there?"

I clenched my fists, anger flaring in my chest. "What are you talking about?"

He sighed, as if disappointed. "You're not here just because of the things you've done, Arlo. You're here because of the person you let yourself become. The person who's too afraid to let go of the past, too afraid to move forward."

"That's not true," I shot back, my voice rising. "I've been facing everything. I've been trying to make it right."

"Have you?" he asked, his tone cutting. "Or have you just been going through the motions, hoping it'll be enough to make the pain go away?"

The words hit me like a punch to the gut because, deep down, I knew there was truth in them. I'd been so focused on fixing the past that I hadn't thought about what came after. About what it meant to truly move on.

"What do you want from me?" I asked, my voice barely audible.

"I want you to stop running," he said simply. "Stop running from the person you are. Stop running from the fact that you're broken. And stop pretending that fixing a few memories is going to make everything better."

I felt tears prick at the corners of my eyes. "I don't know how," I admitted. "I don't know how to stop."

He stepped closer, until he was right in front of me. For the first time, his expression softened. "You don't have to have all the answers, Arlo. You just have to be willing to face the questions."

Slowly, he reached out and placed a hand on my shoulder. The moment he did, a flood of emotion washed over me—grief, anger, fear, and hope all tangled together. It was overwhelming, but it was also freeing.

"This is who you are," he said quietly. "And that's okay."

The mist around us began to dissolve, and I felt a weight lifting from my chest. When I opened my eyes, I was back in the hallway of the Last Chance Hotel. The sixth door was closed behind me, its surface no longer rippling but smooth and still.

Guide was waiting, his expression unreadable. "Well?" he asked.

I took a deep breath, letting it out slowly. "I think I'm finally ready to stop running."

Guide nodded, a faint smile tugging at the corners of his lips. "Good. Because there's only one door left."

I turned to face the final door, its frame glowing faintly in the distance. My heart pounded, but this time, it wasn't fear that drove it. It was something else. Something stronger.

Hope.

THE FINAL DOOR

The door before me was unlike any I had seen in the Last Chance Hotel. It was massive, towering above me, with intricate carvings that shimmered faintly in the dim light. The carvings depicted scenes from my journey: me and Theo in lab coats, working side by side on our dream project; Juniper and me walking together, hand in hand, her light blue highlights catching the sunlight; the school stairwell; the tornado; the couch where Mom and I sat; and the swing set I had once selfishly refused to share. Each moment was etched into the wood, glowing softly, as if alive.

Taking a deep breath, I gripped the handle. It was warm to the touch, pulsing gently beneath my fingers. With one final pull, I stepped through.

I landed on soft grass, the blades cool and damp beneath my hands. The air was crisp, filled with the earthy scent of trees and the faint sweetness of flowers. All around me were towering trees, their canopies stretching into a sky filled with stars. The stars were brilliant, unlike any I had ever seen, and planets hung in the distance like ornaments, glowing with vibrant colors. The serenity of the scene was overwhelming, and for a moment, I forgot why I was there.

I sat down, my knees folding beneath me as I stared up at the cosmos. A part of me wanted to stay here forever. This place felt like peace, like closure. But deep down, I knew this wasn't the end—not yet.

A shift in the air made me look up. The stars dimmed, and the planets seemed to retreat as a shadow spread across the sky. Then, out of nowhere, he appeared. The Guide.

But this wasn't the Guide I had grown accustomed to. He wasn't his usual, human-like self. He was colossal, larger than a planet, his form stretching across the heavens. His face, though familiar, was now ageless and stern, his eyes glowing with an intensity that pierced through me. His voice boomed, shaking the very ground I sat on.

"So, Arlo," he said, his voice reverberating like thunder. "On this journey of yours, what have you learned?"

I stood, my legs trembling beneath me, but I forced myself to meet his gaze. "Honestly, my life was miserable because I made it that way," I said, my voice steady despite the enormity of him. "It's like people say: life is what you make it. I sat in my misery for so long that I forgot how to live. I missed out on opportunities, love, and friendships because it was easier to blame my misery on everything else. I should have tried harder. I wish I had tried harder. Maybe I wouldn't be dead right now."

I paused, taking a deep breath. "That said, I'm glad I went through those painful memories. Seeing the outcomes when I changed things made me feel better. Maybe, just maybe, another Arlo in another universe gets to live the life I kept myself from living. Regardless of my bad decisions, I've found peace. I've accepted the life I lived, and I'm ready to leave it behind."

The Guide's glowing eyes narrowed as he leaned closer, his presence overwhelming. "You've faced your memories, Arlo. But before you pass through the gate, there is one final challenge."

The ground beneath me trembled as the Guide raised a hand, and the serene landscape around me began to twist and change.

The trees dissolved into smoke, the stars above were swallowed by darkness, and the soft grass turned into jagged stone. I was no longer in a peaceful meadow—I was standing on the edge of a crumbling cliff, the abyss below swirling with shadow.

The Guide's voice boomed again. "You've confronted your regrets, but now you must confront *me*. Prove to me that you've truly learned to fight for what matters."

A flash of light blinded me, and when I opened my eyes, I was holding a sword. It was sleek and gleaming, its blade etched with the same carvings that had adorned the final door. My heart raced as I felt a surge of energy course through me. I looked down and saw that I had wings—brilliant, shimmering wings that seemed to hum with power.

The Guide extended his hand, and from the swirling abyss below, a massive spear emerged, dark and crackling with energy. "Come, Arlo," he said, his voice a mix of challenge and encouragement. "Show me your resolve."

I didn't have time to think. The Guide thrust his spear, and a shockwave rippled toward me. Instinct took over as I spread my wings and leaped into the air, dodging the attack. I flew toward him, gripping the sword tightly, and swung with all my might. The blade met his spear, and the clash sent sparks flying, illuminating the darkened void around us.

The battle was unlike anything I could have imagined. The Guide moved with impossible speed for someone so large, each strike of his spear sending waves of energy that shattered the ground beneath me. I darted through the air, my wings carrying me higher and faster than I thought possible. With every swing of my sword, I could feel my strength growing, my resolve solidifying.

"Is that all you've got?" the Guide taunted, his voice echoing around me. "You claim to have learned, but can you truly let go of your pain?"

His words struck a nerve, but I channeled the emotion into my next attack. I dove toward him, the blade of my sword glowing brighter as I focused all my energy into a single strike. The Guide raised his spear to block, but this time, my blade cut through the dark energy surrounding it. The impact sent both of us reeling.

I landed on the ground, breathing hard. The Guide stood, his massive form flickering as though it were unstable. He looked down at me, and for the first time, I saw something in his eyes that hadn't been there before: approval.

"You've done well, Arlo," he said, his voice softer now. "You fought not out of anger or regret, but out of a desire to move forward. That is the mark of someone ready to leave their past behind."

The jagged cliff and swirling abyss faded away, replaced by the serene meadow I had first landed in. The sword in my hand disappeared, and my wings dissolved into light. The Guide returned to his usual, human-like form, stepping closer to me.

"This is where we part ways," he said. "You've passed the Last Chance Hotel in my book. It's time for you to move on to the next journey."

The world around me turned white, and when the light faded, I was back on the path leading to the gate. The robed man stood at the entrance, waiting for me. I turned to look behind me, hoping to catch one last glimpse of the Last Chance Hotel, but it was gone.

Taking a deep breath, I walked toward the gate, ready to embrace whatever came next.

THE AFTERLIFE

The man in robes stood at the gate, his expression calm and unchanging. His presence felt lighter now, less imposing than before, as though the weight of judgment had finally lifted.

"You made it through the Last Chance Hotel," he said, his voice steady and warm. "You may pass through the gate now."

I took a deep breath, the weight of the journey settling in my chest. Every regret I'd confronted, every memory I'd relived, every piece of my soul I'd wrestled with—it had all led to this moment. My hand reached out, trembling slightly, and pushed the gate open.

The air shifted as I stepped through, and what I saw took my breath away.

I was no longer bound to the world I had known. This place was an entirely new plane of existence, shimmering with an ethereal beauty that felt both foreign and familiar. The sky stretched endlessly, painted in hues of lavender, gold, and deep cerulean, as though it were in a perpetual twilight. The breeze carried with it a fragrance unlike anything I'd ever known—a blend of blooming flowers, fresh rain, and something indescribably pure.

I looked down at my arms and realized I was no longer in my human form. My body was translucent, a soft, glowing light radiating from within. I was spirit now, unburdened by flesh and bone, and yet I felt more alive than ever before.

The land stretched out before me, a vibrant tapestry of life. Trees of every imaginable color—from emerald green to crimson red and even shimmering silver—swayed gently in the breeze. The grass beneath me was soft, swaying slightly as if alive, and the air itself seemed to hum with harmony.

Animal spirits roamed freely across the land—majestic stags with antlers that glowed like moonlight, birds with feathers that shimmered like gemstones, and even creatures I couldn't name but felt no fear of. They moved with purpose, yet their energy was calm, as though they too were at peace.

In the distance, I saw human spirits gathered around a glowing campfire. They were laughing, their voices carrying warmth and joy. Some were seated, exchanging stories, while others danced barefoot in the soft grass. Their forms glowed faintly, but their individuality shone through—their features distinct, their personalities vibrant. There was no sign of conflict, no trace of greed or hatred. It was humanity as it was meant to be—united, free, and at peace.

I continued to walk, taking it all in. A young girl caught my eye. She was running through a meadow, throwing a stick for a lion to chase. The massive creature bounded after it, its golden mane flowing in the wind. The lion returned, dropping the stick at her feet, and she laughed, her voice a melody that seemed to resonate with the very air. I couldn't help but smile at the sight.

As I walked further, a figure approached me. He was a young man with a wide grin and a bright mohawk that seemed to glow faintly at the tips. He was dressed casually, his energy relaxed and inviting.

"Hey, dude," he said, extending a hand. "You must be new around here. I'm Jerry. Welcome to the afterlife, man!"

I laughed, shaking his hand. "Thanks. I'm Arlo."

Jerry grinned wider. "Well, Arlo, let me be the first to say you've made it to a good place. Take your time, explore, and get to know people. There's no rush here. That's kind of the point."

"It's beautiful," I said, my voice barely above a whisper. "I didn't know something like this was possible."

Jerry nodded, his expression softening. "Yeah, it's something, isn't it? The funny thing is, this place isn't just about what it looks like. It's about what it feels like. Peace, connection, freedom from all the stuff that weighed you down. You'll find that here."

I looked around again, letting his words sink in. The air seemed to hum with understanding, and for the first time in what felt like forever, I truly believed I was free.

"So, what happens now?" I asked.

Jerry shrugged, a playful glint in his eye. "Whatever you want, man. There's no agenda, no expectations. You've done the hard part. Now, you just... be."

I nodded, a sense of calm washing over me. Jerry clapped me on the shoulder. "You're gonna love it here, Arlo. If you need anything, just holler. Otherwise, enjoy. This is your afterlife now."

He gave me a wave and walked off, joining a group of spirits near the campfire. I stood there for a while, watching the way they laughed, the way the light of the fire reflected in their eyes. They weren't just existing—they were living, in a way that I hadn't truly understood until now.

I took another deep breath, the air filling my lungs like a gentle embrace. For so long, I had been weighed down by regret, by guilt, by the choices I had made and the chances I had missed. But here, in this place, all of that melted away. This was peace. This was freedom.

And as I walked further into the afterlife, I felt something I hadn't felt in a long time: hope. Not for what had been, but for what could be. Because here, in this infinite expanse of beauty and connection, I wasn't alone. And I never would be again.

The End

Message from the Author

Dear Reader,

Thank you for joining me on Arlo's journey through the Last Chance Hotel. Writing this story was not just an exploration of a fictional world—it was also a reflection of the struggles, regrets, and triumphs that we all experience in our lives.

Each of us carries our own doors, holding memories we'd rather not revisit, moments of heartbreak, mistakes, and missed chances. But what if we dared to confront them? What if we allowed ourselves to look back, not with fear or shame, but with the courage to understand and grow? That's what this story is about: finding the strength to face the hardest parts of ourselves, and in doing so, learning to let go, forgive, and heal.

Arlo's journey reminds us that life is messy and imperfect, and sometimes we are our own greatest obstacle. But it also shows us that it's never too late to change—to rewrite the narrative we tell ourselves, to make peace with our past, and to embrace the possibility of a brighter future.

If there's one thing I hope you take away from this book, it's this: life is fleeting, but it's also full of opportunities to grow, to love, and to connect. Don't let regrets weigh you down. Instead, use them as stepping stones toward becoming the person you want to be. Forgive yourself, cherish the people who matter, and never stop striving to live fully in the moment.

Remember, even when it feels like all the doors are closed, there's always a way forward. You just have to be brave enough to take the first step.

With gratitude and hope,
Isaiah Young

ABOUT AUTHOR

Isaiah Young is a young book author who strives to bring his creative mind into his stories. He is originally from New York but currently lives in Virginia with his wife. He used to write stories in his theater class in high school and when he got to college he realized that maybe he should start sharing his writings through books. He is a now college graduate whose major is in Communications. Isaiah loves his passion for writing and he also has a strong passion for traveling and going on adventures. He has visited Costa Rica and New Zealand so far and plans to see more places around the world. Join Isaiah on his journey of adventures and stories to be told.

Isaiah Young's Social Media